THE QUEEN'S BEASTS

Published in Great Britain by
Eye Books Limited
29 Barrow Street
Much Wenlock
TF13 6EN
United Kingdom

0203 239 3027

email: info@eye-books.com

A catalogue record for this book is available from
the British Library.

ISBN 9781903070840

Printed by Ozgraf

THE QUEEN'S BEASTS

SOPHIE BRISTOW
ILLUSTRATED BY SOPHIE GLOVER

Lizzie lived in a cottage in Kew Gardens with her father, the park keeper.

During the day, the Gardens were busy.
People strolled around snapping
photographs and admiring the plants.

But in the evening, when the visitors had left, Lizzie had the Gardens all to herself.

After the gates were locked,
she loved to run off and play in
her favourite places.

Every evening she said good night to her friends, the
Queen's Beasts: ten statues, which stood in a line
outside the Palm House.

E GREYHOUND OF   YALE OF BEAUFORT   D DRAGON OF WAL   ITE HORSE OF HANO   LION OF ENGLA

Lizzie touched each one as she ran past.
'Good night, Lion of England,' she shouted,
'good night, Dragon of Wales!'

Sometimes she thought about kissing the Beasts good night, but some of them had fierce teeth, and others had sharp claws or wild eyes.

But one cold, damp evening, Lizzie thought the Beasts looked sad, so she decided to be brave.

Then she heard her father calling, so without kissing them all, she ran home.

A few days later, as Lizzie was leaving the Palm House, she heard a deep, velvety voice.

'Lizzie!' it called.

She looked around, but there was nobody there.

'Over here!' said the voice.

It was coming from a litter bin.

'I can't get out,' said the voice.

Carefully, Lizzie bent to
reach inside.

She felt something cold jump
onto her hand: an empty,
metal drinks can.

'Ugh,' said Lizzie, dropping the can,
which was sticky and smelled bad.

'Ouch!' said the voice, 'that hurt!' The
can wriggled away from her.

'Wait! I'm sorry,' said Lizzie. 'What …
who are you?'

'I'm the Lion of England,'
said the voice.
'I've been stuck in that statue for
years, but now I'm free!'

'You don't look like a Lion,' said Lizzie.

'No,' said the Lion's voice, sadly, 'that's why we need your help.'

'We?' said Lizzie.

Just then, she saw shapes moving towards her. More metal cans, shuffling along the path.

'Don't be afraid, Lizzie,' said another voice.

'I am the Unicorn of Scotland. We've been hoping you'd come and help us.'

'But, I don't understand,' said Lizzie, 'what can I do?'

'We need more empty drinks cans,' replied the Unicorn's voice, 'and strong, sharp scissors. We need to make ourselves new bodies.'

'I'll see what I can do,' said Lizzie, frowning.

The next day, Lizzie collected as many
empty drinks cans
as she could find.

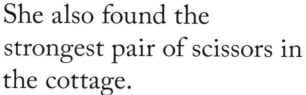

She also found the
strongest pair of scissors in
the cottage.

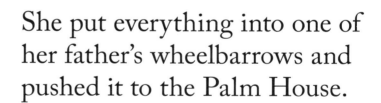

She put everything into one of
her father's wheelbarrows and
pushed it to the Palm House.

'Hello?' Lizzie called, 'is anybody there?'

But there was no reply.

'Must have been a dream,' she shrugged, trudging back to the cottage. But she left the cans and scissors behind, just in case.

The following afternoon, her father
asked about the missing scissors.

'Have you seen them?'

Lizzie ran to the Palm House to
fetch them.

She found the scissors, but the cans had gone.

'Hello?' called Lizzie, shivering.

'Over here!'

There was a rustle in a hedge, and when Lizzie turned,
the face of a lion emerged. Lizzie stepped back.

'Don't worry, I won't bite,' said the Lion.

His muzzle was formed from silvery strips of metal. He licked his lips with a shiny, red tongue.

'Thank you for bringing the cans,' continued the Lion. 'We've been cutting and bending them into new shapes.'

As the Lion spoke, Lizzie heard another rustle. Slowly, more of the Queen's Beasts emerged from the hedge.

No longer stone statues: now, they were glittering and alive.

'But there are only five of you… where are the others?' asked Lizzie.

'Still trapped in stone,' said the Lion, bowing his head.

'Oh!' said Lizzie. 'We must help them to escape… but now, I need to go home, I'm late.'

'Wait!' said the Lion. 'There is one more thing.'

Lizzie stopped.

'We've been listening to people talking in the Gardens.'

'They're saying it's sixty years since the Queen's Coronation. That's why we were made, you see. I remember when we stood outside Westminster Abbey as she rode past in her golden carriage. She was so young and beautiful ….'

'And we were wondering,' said the Unicorn, 'if we might be able to see her again? After all, we are the Queen's Beasts.'

Lizzie laughed.

'You can't just go and see the Queen,' she said, 'it's not that simple.'

The Beasts sighed and hung their heads.

The next day, Lizzie collected more empty cans.
When the visitors had left, she ran to the Palm
House with her wheelbarrow.

The Lion of England was standing by the pond, gazing at the reflection
of his glittering metal body.

'Hello, Lizzie!' he called. 'Like my new crown?' he said, lifting a paw to straighten it.

Lizzie laughed as she saw the Unicorn of Scotland trotting across the lawn, followed by the White Horse of Hanover.

The Falcon and the Dragon were perched on top of the Palm House. As she watched, they spread their wings and glided down to her.

'You're finished!' said Lizzie, as they landed. The Dragon turned his head away and mumbled something from behind his wing.

'Pardon?' said Lizzie, stepping towards him.

'I said don't come any closer!' said the Dragon, a plume of fire shooting from his mouth. He coughed and flapped his wing to clear the smoke.

Lizzie yelped and jumped back from the flame.

'Wait here,' she said, running towards the Palm House.

Lizzie returned with a fire extinguisher.

'Here,' she said, gingerly placing it near the Dragon. 'You might need this.'

The Dragon picked it up, examined it, and then tucked it under his wing with a sigh of relief.

'I'm glad you're finished,' said Lizzie, 'because I have something to tell you.'

The Beasts gathered round her.

'Tomorrow, I am taking you to see the Queen,' said Lizzie. They stared at her with open mouths.

'Thank you, Lizzie, but I'm afraid we can't,' said the Lion, shaking his head. 'Not without the others,' he continued, nodding towards the statues. 'It wouldn't be fair.'

'Oh,' said Lizzie, 'we still need to release the other Beasts, don't we? Do you know any magic words?' She gazed at the statues and stroked her chin.

'Alakazam!' she tried.

'Abracadabra!' she shouted.

'What about rubbing them, like a genie's lamp?'

YALE OF BEAUFOR

But nothing happened. The statues stood and stared.

'Oh, I don't know how to do it,' cried Lizzie, her eyes filling with tears.

'Don't worry,' said the Lion, nuzzling her cheek. 'We don't mind not seeing the Queen. She wouldn't recognise us, anyway.'

Suddenly, a smile crept across Lizzie's face.

'That's it!' cried Lizzie, hugging the Lion's silver mane.

'I know how to release them…' she continued, running towards the Griffin of Edward III.

She tried to ignore his sharp beak and stony scales as she closed her eyes, leaned forward … and kissed him.

'It must have happened that evening in the rain. I felt sorry for you, all cold and wet, so I kissed you goodnight.

'Well, some of you, anyway … before my father called.'

Lizzie and the Beasts stared at the Griffin's statue, hoping for a sign of life. Suddenly, Lizzie heard a tinny rattle, coming from the wheelbarrow.

On the top of the pile, a can wiggled.

'Griffin?' said Lizzie. 'Is that you?'

'Yes,' croaked a voice, 'Griffin here. Thank you Lizzie.'

The can clattered down the pile as he spoke.

'I wondered when you'd realise,' he continued.

'I heard the sculptor muttering to himself while he chipped away at our stone. If somebody with the Queen's name kissed us, we'd be released.'

Lizzie laughed and ran along the line of statues, kissing them. As she did so, four more cans started to wiggle in the wheelbarrow.

'I must go, it's getting late,' said Lizzie. 'There are plenty of cans there for your new bodies. Meet me tomorrow, just before midday. Hide in the woods near the river.'

In the morning, Lizzie helped her father plant geraniums. As midday approached, she slipped away and ran towards the river.

She picked her way through the brambles, hoping that the Beasts would be waiting.

'Hello?' she whispered. 'Anybody here?'

Something glinted from the middle of a holly bush and then a familiar face emerged.

'Lion!' she shouted, throwing her arms around his neck.

Then Lizzie saw the others:
she counted ten, magnificent
metal Beasts, sparkling in the
dappled light.

'Follow me,' said Lizzie, picking her way towards the river.

'Where are we going?' said the Unicorn, trotting to catch up. 'I thought we were going to see the Queen?'

'We are,' said Lizzie as they reached the water's edge. 'You'll see.'

She waved to a woman who was steering a narrowboat towards the riverbank.

The woman's eyes widened as she saw the Beasts, but then she smiled.

'This is my friend, Jill' said Lizzie, catching a rope and pulling the boat towards the bank.

'Today's the day of the Queen's Diamond Jubilee River Pageant. And you, dear Beasts, are going to be in it,' said Lizzie. Gingerly, the Beasts stepped onto the boat and lined up along the flat roof.

As they headed down the river, other boats appeared up ahead, adorned with flags and bunting.

'If you stay still, people will think you're sculptures,' said Lizzie.

'At least there's very little risk of fire,' said the Dragon, surveying the water and clutching his extinguisher.

They sailed under bridges full of crowds of smiling people, who waved flags and cheered as the Beasts glided past.

Further along the river, bells rang out from a floating belfry, and as they passed Westminster Abbey, its bells pealed in reply.

Then Lizzie spotted the Royal Barge, swagged in red velvet.

'There she is!' she shouted, pointing towards a golden pagoda at the front. There stood a small figure with a pale blue hat, turning to the crowds and waving.

'Remember, you're sculptures,' said Lizzie to the Beasts. 'No talking or moving!'

But it was too late. As Lizzie turned, she saw all ten Beasts hopping around and waving either hooves, paws or wings at the Queen. A gasp rose from the crowd along the riverbank.

Slowly, the Queen turned too, until she was staring at the boat with ten metal Beasts dancing on the roof, and a small girl on the front deck.

Lizzie held her breath and gripped the edge of the boat. And then, to her relief, the Queen's mouth curved into a wide smile. Perhaps, Lizzie thought, it was the same smile the Beasts remembered from sixty years ago, as she arrived at the Abbey in her golden coach.

And ever since the Beasts – the Lion of England, the Griffin of Edward III, the Falcon of the Plantagenets, the Black Bull of Clarence, the White Lion of Mortimer, the Yale of Beaufort, the White Greyhound of Richmond, the Red Dragon of Wales, the Unicorn of Scotland and the White Horse of Hanover – have lived in Kew Gardens, hiding during the day but roaming freely at night. And if you ever happen to meet them, they will tell you that, on the day of the Jubilee River Pageant, they made the Queen smile.

This story is based on original artworks of
the Queen's Beasts created by
Tom Hiscocks. For information
www.tomhiscocks.co.uk

Every Can Counts helps recycle drinks cans outside the home. One in every three drinks cans sold in the UK is drunk outside the home. These cans are endlessly recyclable, and it's important they are.

We might be in the habit of recycling at home, but it's not as easy to find recycling points when we're on the go. Every Can Counts has been developed by the drinks can manufacturing and recycling industry to address this

In 2011 they helped organisations save more than 51 million drinks cans: that's over 700 tonnes of aluminium and steel saved for recycling – and more than 5800 tonnes of CO_2 emissions avoided. Users didn't just find their drinks cans recycling improved, the impact of the programme boosted collections of other recyclables, like paper and plastic.

For more information see www.everycancounts.co.uk

These figures were bought to our attention by Ball Packaging Europe, a sponsor of Every Can Counts.